Praise for *Walks Alone*

"*Walks Alone* is nothing less than a song about the struggle for freedom. Burks's language is vigorous and forceful; the story tragic and believable. I knew and mourned for Walks Alone. I heartily recommend this book." —Karen Cushman, author of *The Midwife's Apprentice* and *Catherine, Called Birdy*

"A brutally effective portrayal of the realities of the destruction of Native American culture." —*Kirkus Reviews*

"Burks's attention to historical detail and authenticity makes *Walks Alone* a classic of western historical fiction. It's impossible not to love the courage and drive of this girl." —Gary Paulsen, author of *Dogsong* and *Hatchet*

"Powerful . . . An obvious selection for historical fiction assignments." —*Booklist*

"This is a powerful novel with a heroine of enduring spirit. . . . No punches are pulled." —*VOYA*

WALKS ALONE

BRIAN BURKS

WALKS ALONE

—◆—✦—◆—

HARCOURT, INC.

San Diego   New York   London

Requests for permission to make copies of any part
of the work should be mailed to the following address:
Permissions Department, Harcourt, Inc.,
6277 Sea Harbor Drive, Orlando, Florida 32887-6777.

www.harcourt.com

First Harcourt Paperbacks edition 2000

The Library of Congress has cataloged the hardcover as follows:
Burks, Brian.
Walks Alone/by Brian Burks.
p.   cm.
Summary: After a surprise attack leaves many of her people dead,
fifteen-year-old Walks Alone, an Apache girl wounded in the massacre,
struggles to survive and rejoin the refugee band.
1. Apache Indians—Juvenile fiction.   [1. Apache Indians—Fiction.
2. Indians of North America—Southwest, New—Fiction.
3. Southwest, New—Fiction.   4. Survival—Fiction.]   I. Title.
PZ7.B9235Wal   1998
[Fic]—dc21   97-14738
ISBN 0-15-201612-0
ISBN 0-15-202472-7 pb

Text set in Fairfield
Designed by Linda Lockowitz

A C E G H F D B
Printed in the United States of America

To my children:
Alex, Justin, Tami, Leandra, and Carl

I will not go to San Carlos.
I will not take my people there. We prefer
to die in our own land under the tall, cool pines.
We will leave our bones with those of our people.
It is better to die fighting than to starve—
I have spoken.

—Victorio
1825–1880

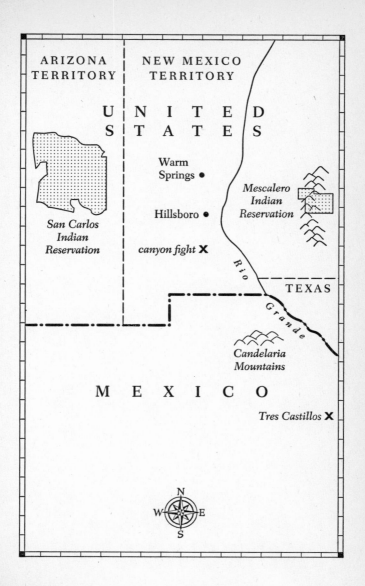

PROLOGUE

※✦※

FOR MANY YEARS Mimbres Apache chief Victorio sought peace with the U.S. government. All he asked was that he and his people be allowed to return to a reservation located in the heart of their Warm Springs ancestral homeland. Just as his efforts were about to succeed, he received word that he was wanted by the authorities for murder and theft.

Believing he would be executed if captured, in 1879 Victorio gathered his band of followers and fled the Mescalero Indian Reservation, to which they had been temporarily assigned. His movements were slowed by women, children, and the aged, whom he refused to leave behind. His warriors were often poorly equipped and half-starved. Yet for one year Victorio waged war, outwitting, outmaneuvering, and outfighting both the American and Mexican armies.

In their relentless struggle for freedom, all of Victorio's people suffered. Some more than others.

WALKS
ALONE

CHAPTER ONE

＊—✦—＊

WALKS ALONE placed one foot on either side of a tangled nest of twigs, leaves, and grass. She raised the sticks in her hands, a long slender one in the left and a shorter, heavier one in the right.

Her heart pounded. When the wood rat ran from the nest, she must not miss it. Her family was hungry. No one had eaten since yesterday, and what little mesquite bean meal and dried yucca fruit they'd had in their buckskin food bags was gone.

Walks Alone poked the slender stick into the top of the nest. A blur of fur raced out. She swung the stick in her right hand. The blow caught the rat just above the tail, wounding it. Quickly she pulled her knife from the badgerskin sheath on her belt, caught the flopping rat by its hind legs, and thrust the blade into its throat.

She straightened up, holding the rat in both hands, and turned to face the east. The morning sun had not yet tipped above the horizon.

"Life Giver," she prayed, "I know that you have helped me. I do not forget you. May you always provide me with food."

A breeze blew, kicking up a dusty whirlwind in the distance. Walks Alone watched the turbulent spiral until it vanished, wondering if it could be a sign of some sort. Unable to grasp its meaning, if there was one, she turned and started for camp. Although she was certain they wouldn't say anything about it, her mother and grandmother were going to be pleased with the fresh meat.

She topped a sandy, barren ridge. Camp lay below, in a narrow box canyon with a spring-fed pool in the bed of it. She had been here before. Whenever the White Eyes' army was getting too close, Victorio brought the people here to hide and to rest.

Sometimes, depending on how many warriors were out on raids and whether or not the band had split up into smaller parties to avoid capture, the group of Warm Springs Apaches numbered three hundred or more. Today, fewer than half that many were here.

As Walks Alone drew closer, she noticed a lone warrior standing on a large rock at the northern edge of the camp. Although it was too far to tell much about him, she quickly recognized the Apache chief Victorio. His Indian name was Bidu-ya, meaning the Conqueror, but most everyone knew him by his Spanish name, Victorio.

She gazed at the man while continuing at her brisk pace. Like most Apaches, Victorio was brown-eyed, short, and compact. But no one who had seen his broad face could easily forget it. It was powerful, with thin lips, a full nose, pronounced cheeks, and a heavy, firm-set lower jaw. The chief rarely wore any ornaments, paint, or feathers, yet Walks Alone thought he was the most magnificent human being she had ever seen.

Victorio was loved and admired by almost all of the Warm Springs Apaches. He was wise and brave and honest, and he was determined to fight the White Eyes until he and his people were allowed to return to their homeland at Warm Springs—or until he died.

Walks Alone entered the camp. Because the band of Indians was constantly on the move and had arrived in the canyon just last night, no wickiups or brush arbors had been built. Some of the families had blankets to sit or lie on, but others had only the ground. No one owned more than they could carry on a horse or on their backs.

A group of children was playing, attempting to dig out a gopher hole. A long-haired, flat-faced boy spotted Walks Alone and rushed toward her. He had almost reached her when he tripped and fell. She helped him up.

"My small brother." She smiled. "How are you going to become a mighty warrior if you cannot keep your legs under you?"

Sleeps In A Bush wiped at his snotty nose, then reached for the rat in her free hand. Walks Alone held it away from him and walked to where her mother and grandmother were sitting. They had built a fire out of dry mesquite wood. Hot coals had been raked to the side, and part of the crown of a sotol plant had been placed there to roast. This fire, along with the others in the camp, made almost no smoke. Soldiers could be nearby and everyone was cautious not to alert them to the camp's location.

Walks Alone laid the rat on the coals beside the sotol. Sometimes she skinned the rats and removed the entrails before cooking, but they tasted just as good and were easier to skin if baked whole first.

She looked at her mother, who was seated by the fire. Snow On Her had large, dark eyes, an

4

oval, small-nosed face, and a plump, full body. She was considered quite pretty. Her husband, Two Horns, had died a year earlier, while on a raid against white settlers. According to custom, she was then bound to marry her husband's brother. Because Two Horns had no brother, she was obligated to his cousins.

There was only one cousin who was not already married, and because he was just seventeen—two years older than Walks Alone—the family had not forced the marriage and had given Snow On Her freedom. Several braves had vied for her attention without success. If Snow On Her ever intended to marry again, she gave no indication of it.

Snow On Her stood. Her expression was grave. She gestured at the thin, heavily wrinkled woman who was still sitting, busily threading a piece of rawhide through the sole of a moccasin.

"Your grandmother thinks it is time for you to have a husband. She says she wants to see her great-grandchildren before she is gone. She says she is going to send word to Round Nose's relatives that he can have you for three good horses and two soft buckskins."

Walks Alone's face turned pale. It was customary for the relatives of a young Apache maiden to arrange her marriage, sometimes without even telling her about the match until all the arrangements had been made. But Walks Alone had other plans for her life.

She moved to face her grandmother across the fire and started to speak. But she knew she was too upset to choose her words carefully. She knelt, staring at the ground until she had calmed. Finally she raised her head.

"My grandmother, I know your years are many and that you are wise. I know you will do what is best for me. But Round Nose is twice my age. I do not love him."

"Love." The elderly woman grunted, looking up from her task for the first time. "Love is not for you. It is for foolish girls. Will love fill your empty belly? Will it provide you and your children with clothes to wear? Round Nose is a wealthy man. He has many horses. He is from a family of standing. He will be a great help to us."

Walks Alone understood what her grandmother was referring to. The man Walks Alone married would be responsible not only for her needs but for those of her relatives as well. He would be required to leave his family and live with hers.

"My grandmother." Walks Alone's voice was soft. "You have taught me that a marriage is no good if it does not last. I ask you not to send word to Round Nose. There is another whom I care for."

"You speak of that skinny boy, Little Hawk."
The woman stretched the length of the moccasin
sole. "I have seen the two of you together. He has
no present to offer. He does not own anything. He
would be of no help to us. With him there would
be no meat on our fire and your children would go
around naked in the winter."

Anger stirred in Walks Alone. She inched backward on her knees to get away from the heat of the
fire. Again she paused to master her emotions.

"You know that I will do whatever you say. I ask
you to wait for one harvest. Little Hawk is a good
hunter. He has great skill with the bow. He has
finished his fourth training raid and he is a man
now. He is a warrior. Soon he will have many
horses."

Snow On Her stepped beside the old woman
and sat down, folding her legs beneath her. She
gazed into the distance at the canyon walls while
she spoke.

"For months we have been running. More of
the White Eyes are hunting us than ever before.
We do not know when the fighting will stop. We
do not know if we will ever be able to go back to
our home at Warm Springs. The people are hungry. They are tired. It is not a good time for babies
to be born."

7

Sleeps In A Bush crawled into his mother's lap. Snow On Her brushed sand off the boy's cheeks and hands while Walks Alone anxiously awaited her grandmother's decision.

At last the elderly woman spoke. "I will wait."

Walks Alone scrambled to her feet. She hugged her grandmother and then her mother. Snow On Her held up Sleeps In A Bush. "Take him. Bring some water."

The intestine of a deer, which they used for a canteen, was hung on a nearby greasewood branch. Walks Alone shifted her brother to one hip, took the canteen, and jogged through camp toward the streambed. Her spirits were high and she felt so light it seemed almost unnecessary for her feet to touch the ground.

She reached the small, shallow pool, set Sleeps In A Bush on a flat rock, and laid the intestine in the water.

Walks Alone squeezed the intestine to get the air out and allow the water to flow in. As she did, she noticed her reflection in the ripples. It had been a long time since she had last seen herself, so long that she couldn't remember when or where that was.

The water became still and the clear reflection startled her. It looked as if her mother were in the water, looking up at her. Walks Alone stroked her chin, then touched her nose. Yes, the reflection was hers.

A shadow caught Walks Alone's attention and she turned her head to see Little Hawk approaching. Like most warriors, he wore only a broad loincloth made of buckskin that fell in front to right above his knees and hung lower in back, just high enough that he wouldn't step on it.

He knelt a respectful distance from her and scooped a handful of water to his mouth. She knew he was using his thirst for an excuse to be near her. Open courtship among young people was strictly forbidden, and times like this were the only chances they had to meet. Whenever Little Hawk was placed on sentry duty outside the camp, Walks Alone had trouble finding firewood anywhere except in the area where he was standing watch.

She remembered her grandmother's words and quickly glanced over Little Hawk's lithe body. Perhaps he could stand a little more weight, but he wasn't skinny. His brown arms and legs were thick and strong, his chest broad and deep.

He looked her way and she busied herself, skimming the water into the open end of the already full intestine.

"I hope we can stay in this place for a while," he said. "I am going hunting today. If Life Giver

9

and Crow provide me with a deer or antelope, I can give it to whomever I want."

"Yes," she answered. "It will be yours."

"I want to give it to you."

She smiled, remembering her grandmother's statement about no meat on the fire. "May the deer and the antelope not be afraid of you."

Two women approached the pool. Little Hawk saw them and rose to leave.

Then suddenly a gunshot boomed, ripping apart the morning calm. One of the two women fell. Walks Alone jumped to her feet, looking for Sleeps In A Bush. She could see him nowhere.

More shots thundered, quickly growing to a steady, deafening roar that echoed loudly against the canyon walls.

Walks Alone started running, searching frantically for her brother. Little Hawk dashed by, throwing Sleeps In A Bush into her arms.

"The arroyo! Run!"

Walks Alone understood. The streambed below the rock shelf that held this pool had been cut deep by centuries of floodwater. If she could reach it, the high walls would provide protection.

She rushed for it, pushing herself faster and faster. The edge of the ravine was close when a bullet tugged at the upper part of her left leg, knocking it out from under her. She managed to hold Sleeps In A Bush above her as she fell, sliding across an outcrop of barren, jagged rock. The rock tore her buckskin dress and cut at her flesh.

Determined to push on, Walks Alone scrambled forward on her bare knees. She reached the arroyo edge and slid over, landing on her feet. A bolt of pain shot from her wounded leg, and her vision blurred. Dizziness washed over her and she leaned against the arroyo bank to steady herself.

Shouts came from above. Screams. The gunfire thickened. Walks Alone gritted her teeth. She had to move, had to run. If she got caught where she was, the steep arroyo walls that she had hoped would protect her would become a trap with no way out.

She took a step, then another. The pain was shocking, but the injured leg held her weight. She forced herself into a jog, gradually increasing speed. In time the sounds of the battle were behind her.

With Sleeps In A Bush held tightly against her chest, she ran until her heaving lungs could take no more. Then she stopped and hid under a gnarled salt cedar tree that had grown between a boulder and one side of the arroyo.

Her strength was gone. Occasionally a distant

gunshot could be heard, but it sounded as if the fighting was nearly over.

Walks Alone hoped her mother, her grand-mother, and Little Hawk were all right. She set her brother on the ground beside her and looked down at her wounded leg.

It was covered in blood.

CHAPTER TWO

——◄═◊═►——

IT WAS APACHE SCOUTS, working for the White
Eyes' army, who had attacked the camp. Walks
Alone was sure of it. No one else could have
slipped close enough to make the ambush without
being seen or heard.

She despised the scouts. They were traitors. If
it weren't for their skills in tracking and fighting,
the White Eyes would have been helpless.

Walks Alone leaned against the arroyo bank,
straightening her injured leg. Fortunately the bullet had missed the bone, going completely through
the flesh behind it. She managed to stop the bleeding by packing the wound with dry buffalo grass
and wrapping it with a strip of buckskin she cut

from the side of her dress. The pain was severe, but so long as she was able to bear it, the leg was usable.

The day was nearly gone. Only a pale, dusky light remained. The last gunshot Walks Alone had heard came sometime before noon. She wanted to leave her hiding place and attempt to make it back to the camp. But that was too dangerous. The scouts could still be around. Perhaps by now the White Eyes had joined them. She would have to wait. Tomorrow would be soon enough.

Sleeps In A Bush snuggled against her, laying his head on her shoulder. She knew he was hungry and thirsty. Neither of them had eaten since yesterday, and they'd had their last drink of water early in the morning, before she killed the rat.

She picked up two round pebbles, put one in her mouth, and handed the boy the other. The stones would start saliva and help to moisten their parched throats.

Walks Alone rested her chin on her chest. She was exhausted. The loss of blood had made her weak. She closed her eyes. Her thoughts drifted to more peaceful times.

At Warm Springs, she and her people had been happy. The sacred spring's water was healthful, especially in the winter. And before the White Eyes came, there were always berries, nuts, fruit, deer, and antelope in the area. There were mountains and valleys, providing plenty of grass and timber. Women and children didn't get sick there, and neither did horses or cattle.

If the White Eyes had only left us alone, she wished. Instead the people had been gathered and put into wagons and taken to a reservation at San Carlos, where some of them died.

San Carlos had been a terrible place where there was nothing but cactus, rattlesnakes, heat, rocks, and insects. Everyone got sick. There were no plants or game to eat. Victorio had known that if the band continued to stay there, no one would live.

Again he took the people back to Warm Springs, and they were happy. But the soldiers came a second time and captured many and forced them back to San Carlos. Victorio fled.

Later, Victorio and the band were allowed to go to the Mescalero Apache reservation near Fort Stanton. It was not as good a place as Warm Springs, but everyone liked it much better than San Carlos. The group of Warm Springs Apaches might have stayed there if Victorio had not heard that white lawmen were going to arrest and kill him for a murder they thought he had committed near Silver City.

Late one night, Victorio woke everyone in

camp and broke out of the reservation. For the last several months now, the band had been running, raiding, and fighting, sometimes crossing the border into Mexico.

Walks Alone was falling asleep. A scene came to her. Her father, Two Horns, was holding her by both hands and swinging her around and around, laughing.

She tried to make the memory go away. It was not good to think about the dead. Their ghosts might come around to haunt you. That was why everything a dead person had owned or used was burned or buried with them. Even their horse was killed. This helped to keep the living from remembering the dead—and those who were gone would need their possessions in the other world.

But Walks Alone had had trouble forgetting. For a long time after her father's death, she'd walked almost every day, keeping to herself. She often paced along the rim of a distant hill, far away from camp. That was why her grandmother had changed her name from Running Deer to Walks Alone.

Walks Alone opened her eyes. She wondered if there would ever be peace again. She longed for a home, a place where she and Little Hawk could marry and raise a family.

Sleeps In A Bush sneezed, and she gently covered his mouth with her hand. The scouts and soldiers could be anywhere. She and her brother must remain silent. Their hiding place must not be found.

CHAPTER THREE

—⊷⊱⊰⊶—

T HE LATE SUMMER SKY was clear and the day
hot. Walks Alone hobbled past the spot where
she had slid into the arroyo at the start of the battle the day before. Her wounded leg was stiff and
swollen. If she hadn't found a piece of driftwood
to use for a cane, she was sure she would never
have made it this far.

Ahead, Sleeps In A Bush was crawling up the
bank to the rock shelf that held the pool of water.
She started to call to him, to tell him to wait for
her, then decided it didn't matter. Getting up the
steep embankment was going to be difficult
enough without trying to help him.

A while later Walks Alone strained to pull herself over the top. Sweat beaded her brow, her breathing was harsh, and her muscles trembled. She saw Sleeps In A Bush lying by the pool, drinking. In the rippling water she could make out two dark forms.

Walks Alone disregarded the pain in her leg and sprang to her feet. She hurried to her brother and picked him up. The pool held the bodies of two dead warriors. She guessed the scouts had thrown them there so they would rot, making the water undrinkable.

The sound of flapping wings startled Walks Alone, and she looked up to see a buzzard circling. She turned toward the camp. There were more buzzards, dozens of them. And there were more bodies.

She tightened her arms around her brother and rushed from one corpse to the next, scaring off the big, ugly birds. Her tears flowed as she recognized the faces of the dead, most of them women and children.

Walks Alone fell to her knees. In front of her lay her mother. Snow On Her's chest was caked with dried blood and her dull brown eyes stared blankly at the sky.

Walks Alone knew she shouldn't make noise, yet her grief was too strong. She wailed loudly. For the moment her safety didn't matter. Her brother's safety did not matter. Nothing mattered.

She set Sleeps In A Bush on the ground, took her knife in one hand, and grabbed a handful of her own long black hair with the other. It was the custom of Apache families to cut their hair when mourning the loss of a close relative. The knife was dull and cutting was hard work, but Walks Alone didn't stop until every strand long enough to grasp was gone.

A slight breeze blew, the air feeling strange against her bare neck. It was unexplainable, but somehow cutting her hair had made her feel better. She sheathed the knife and wiped her eyes. On the ground Sleeps In A Bush had crawled onto his mother's chest, placing his face against hers.

Walks Alone stood and picked the boy up.

"She is gone, my brother. Never again will her name be spoken. No more will our mother be remembered."

Sleeps In A Bush fought against her, reaching out for his mother. Walks Alone moved away. She wondered if any others she loved were among the dead.

CHAPTER FOUR

＋·✦·＋

NIGHT WAS FAST COMING. Walks Alone placed the blunt end of a shaved sotol stalk into a notch she had cut in a flat piece of yucca stalk. The hastily made fire drill wasn't as good as the one her mother had used, but it would do. Everything Snow On Her owned—her fire drill, the rawhide rope she used to carry firewood on her back, her basket, the sewing awl made from the sharpened legbone of a deer, the small clay pot, her food bag, and her knife—Walks Alone had buried with her.

Walks Alone spun the sotol stick between her hands. A thin wisp of smoke rose. She continued to spin the stick until the smoke thickened, then blew on the dry grass piled around it. In moments the grass was ablaze, and she added a few twigs.

Her thoughts were not on the fire but on those she had left behind in the canyon. She was thankful that Little Hawk and her grandmother had not been among the two dozen or more bodies she had found. But the other bodies needed to be buried and it bothered her that she was helpless to do anything for them. With her injured leg, it had taken her most of the day just to find and carry enough rocks to cover her mother.

Afterward she had gone to the streambed above the pool and scooped out a hole in the sand deep enough to allow fresh water to pour in. She and Sleeps In A Bush drank, and she found, cleaned, and filled the deer-intestine canteen she'd left in the pool. Then she butchered the back straps off of a horse that had been killed in the battle, put them over her shoulder, and made her way out of the canyon.

On top of the canyon ridge, she had crossed the trail where Victorio had taken the survivors and fled. Another trail was just as plain: the tracks of the scouts and soldiers who were chasing them.

Walks Alone put a couple of mesquite branches on the fire. The campsite she had chosen was in a low place between two sand hills, where the light from her fire could not be easily seen.

The night darkness was nearly complete. There was no moon. Walks Alone was glad she had left the canyon. It was not good to camp or sleep where someone had died. Their ghost might come around and bother you.

Sleeps In A Bush crawled near the fire. Walks Alone had cut the boy's hair while they were still in the canyon, and he looked strikingly different. She wished she had another loincloth to put on him. Because they had both been in close contact with the dead, they needed to burn their clothes, bathe, and put on something else. But there wasn't any water here for bathing and there was nothing else to wear.

The boy picked up the intestine canteen from the ground. Walks Alone untied the rawhide thong, holding one end shut, and helped him get a drink. It had been hours since they had drunk from the streambed, and she was thirsty, too, but she denied herself. The only water for miles was back in the canyon and she didn't want to go back there—*ever*. What water they had was going to have to last.

Tomorrow she would take Sleeps In A Bush and follow her people's trail. She was sure Victorio had headed for Mexico. Once he crossed the border, a hundred miles to the south, the White Eyes and the scouts would stop chasing him. He would slow down, giving the women and children time to rest. Walks Alone knew that if she persistently followed the trail, she and her brother would eventually rejoin the band.

Her leg throbbed. She removed the buckskin wrap and the grass she had packed in the wound to stop the bleeding. Besides the swelling, the flesh was dark purple where the bullet had entered and exited.

There was only one thing she could think of to do. Her mother had used this treatment on her father, and he had been healed.

She waited until the mesquite branches had burned to embers, then scraped them out and added more wood to the fire so she would have light to see by. She picked up one of the coals between two sticks, gritted her teeth, and placed it on the wound.

Walks Alone's body shook against the pain. The stench of burning flesh was strong. Her eyes were open but she did not see. Her father, Two Horns, was pictured in her mind.

Again she watched his face as her mother placed burning coals on an arrow wound in the man's shoulder. Sweat trickled down his face and his lips were clenched together so tightly they were white. But he did not make a sound. She would make no sound either.

Five more times Walks Alone put embers on her leg. One in the other side of the wound, and four in spots surrounding it. This, she knew, would help the swelling go down. Finished, she rewrapped her leg with the buckskin and lay back on the ground exhausted.

The stars above were bright. A lone coyote howled in the distance, soon joined by the yelping of others. Walks Alone was nearly asleep. She forced herself to sit up and check on the cooking horse meat. As she did, she heard a faint cry.

She looked at Sleeps In A Bush. "Did you hear that?"

The boy nodded, moving closer to her. Something was wrong with Sleeps In A Bush's voice, and since birth he had never uttered a word. His hearing, however, was excellent, and he understood most of what anyone said to him.

In moments the eerie sound came again.

"It is a ghost," Walks Alone whispered. Immediately she was angry with herself for further frightening the boy. Sleeps In A Bush crawled still closer.

Walks Alone wondered if the cry could be coming from her mother. Then she remembered that Snow On Her had been the one who had named her brother. According to custom, his name must now be changed so it would hold no connection to the dead. If their mother was the ghost, and Walks Alone changed the boy's name, the ghost might go away.

She picked up Sleeps In A Bush and turned him around in her lap to look at his face.

"Listen to me," she said. "No longer is your name Sleeps In A Bush. It is . . ."

Walks Alone tried to quickly think of something that would describe her brother. The only thing she could come up with was that because he couldn't talk, he was always quiet.

She continued. "Your name is One Who Is Quiet. Do you understand? From now on, your name is One Who Is Quiet."

The boy nodded and squirmed around, putting his back against her chest.

Changing the name didn't help. The cries and moans continued, growing louder and more frequent.

Walks Alone listened intently. What if the weeping wasn't coming from a ghost? What if one of her people, perhaps a child, was out there— wounded and hurting?

She set One Who Is Quiet beside her and stood, finding the pain in her leg was considerably less than it had been before she'd placed the embers on it. Her exhaustion was gone, replaced by fear and a need to find the source of the cries. She was awake and alert.

Walks Alone took a piece of horse meat off the rock by the fire, finding it still half-raw but edible. Whatever or whoever was out there, she and her brother were near starving. They had to eat to maintain their strength. Then, maybe, they'd venture out.

CHAPTER FIVE

·—◄═◆═►—·

THE TORCH Walks Alone had fashioned out of dry greasewood limbs had not lasted long. She held the end of it near the ground in front of her, taking advantage of what little light its few glowing embers still provided.

She crept on, tightly gripping her brother's hand and stepping past a tall bush that seconds earlier had looked like the silhouette of a man. Except for an occasional moan, the crying had stopped.

Walks Alone's heart was beating rapidly. She knew she had to be getting close to the spot where the cries had come from.

An owl hooted from somewhere ahead. Walks Alone stopped. The owl was a ghost. All owls were ghosts. Whenever a wicked person died, he didn't go to the other world. His spirit entered the body of an owl so he could continue to exercise his evil influence. Owls stayed near places where people had died, and their presence meant someone else was going to die.

Walks Alone forced her shaking legs to turn. She was convinced that there was nothing out here but ghosts and she wanted to get away from them as quickly as her wounded leg would allow.

She took a step. A hand grabbed her ankle. She jerked her leg free and jumped sideways, almost knocking down One Who Is Quiet.

A girl spoke between loud, short breaths. "Help me. Please . . . help me."

Walks Alone held the glowing embers on the end of the torch toward the voice. In the faint light she could see the outline of someone lying on the ground.

"Who are you?"

"I am Gray In Hair." The voice was weak. "My baby . . . my baby will not be born."

Walks Alone was so badly shaken it took a moment for her to place the name with the Mescalero Apache girl who had married a Warm Springs warrior and joined the band nearly a year ago. Gray In Hair was a shy person, and Walks

Alone had had the opportunity to speak with her only a few times.

Gray In Hair gasped and moaned. The agonizing sound was the same one Walks Alone had been hearing. But that didn't explain the presence of the owl. One ghost was surely nearby, and there might be others.

Walks Alone released her brother's hand. The first thing she had to do was use the burning embers on the end of the torch to start a campfire. A big campfire. The danger of scouts or soldiers seeing it was an unavoidable risk. The blaze had to be bright enough so that it would help to keep the ghosts away and also provide plenty of light to see by.

It took a while to gather enough dry limbs, but at last the fire was burning brilliantly. Walks Alone was glad she had brought the intestine canteen. She knelt beside Gray In Hair and helped her take a drink. The girl's sweaty face was drained of color.

"How long have you been hurting?" Walks Alone asked.

"Since . . ." Gray In Hair held her breath against an intense labor pang. "Since before the morning sun."

Gray In Hair's condition was serious, Walks Alone knew. The girl had lost a great deal of blood and she was weak. *Too weak.* If the baby wasn't born soon, both mother and child could die.

Walks Alone scanned the area for a thick, up-right branch. Besides helping her own mother give birth to One Who Is Quiet, she had helped in other deliveries, and with each of them, the expecting woman's hands had been bound or held to a post while she knelt in front of it. This was the way nearly all Apache children came into the world.

A gnarled, dead mesquite trunk about waist high caught Walks Alone's eye, and she went to it, hoping the base wasn't rotten. She found it sturdy enough, and the only work required was breaking off a few limbs.

As Walks Alone removed the limbs and threw them near the fire, she remembered another woman whose baby would not be born. Witchcraft had been the suspected reason for the trouble. The soon-to-be mother had had an argument with another woman a few days earlier and it was believed that a spell had been cast against her and her child.

The woman had been fortunate, though, and an old man who was a shaman arrived to help her. He drew a black cross on his hand with charcoal. Then he put his hand on the woman's stomach and sang a ceremonial song. Before he had finished the third verse, a baby boy was born.

34

A difficult delivery could also be caused by food. If a pregnant woman ate too much meat fat or too many piñon nuts, the child inside her would grow too large. Also, an expecting mother must avoid eating any animal intestines or her baby might get tangled up in—or strangled by—the umbilical cord.

Walks Alone hoped Gray In Hair hadn't been around a witch or eaten the wrong things. There would be no help from a shaman here. Walks Alone was going to have to do the best she could with what little she had and knew.

She stepped back from her work. The post was ready.

She returned to Gray In Hair, wishing she had some salt. Her grandmother had told her that salt, swallowed with warm water and four of the inner leaves of a narrow-leafed yucca bush, would speed up a delivery.

The owl they had heard earlier hooted again. One Who Is Quiet stepped close to his sister. Walks Alone put her hand on his shoulder and pointed to the other side of the fire.

"My brother, I want you to go over there and sit with your back to us. Add wood to the fire when the light grows dim. It will help keep the ghost away. Pray to Life Giver for us. Do not move until I come to you."

Most of the night was gone when Gray In Hair's baby girl cried loudly. Walks Alone gave a sigh of relief and smiled as she laid the newborn on the ground and wiped out its nose and mouth with her fingers so the child could breathe easier.

"Do not move," Walks Alone warned Gray In Hair, picking up her knife from the ground beside her. She pulled the sheath off and felt the edge of the blade, wishing it were sharper. The cord on other babies she had seen born had been cut with a piece of long, black flint or the tapered edge of a length of reed, but Walks Alone had neither. The knife would have to do.

She took the cord in her left hand and, being careful not to force the knife and possibly tear the cord, cut through it. Then she tied the cord into a tight knot that rested against the child's navel.

Walks Alone picked up the still-crying infant. She wanted to wash her, but that would take most of the water they had. She carried the baby around the mesquite trunk for Gray In Hair to see.

"Life Giver has taken pity on you," Walks Alone said softly. "Your baby is fine."

Gray In Hair was so weak she could hardly raise her head. The sight of her child caused the lines in her face to relax.

"Life Giver sent you to me," she said to Walks Alone. "That is how he chose to help me."

Walks Alone held the baby in outstretched arms toward the east. Then she offered her to the south, the west, and the north. By doing this she was acknowledging the spiritual help they had received and was also asking for further protection.

She turned to Gray In Hair. "I will bring you water. You must stay where you are until you are stronger."

Later in the night, Walks Alone eased herself down next to her sleeping brother and glanced at the new baby lying on her mother's chest. The child had straight black hair and a sturdy round body. Her skin needed to be rubbed with animal fat to keep it from drying out and getting sore, but they had none. A blanket was needed to wrap her in, but they didn't have that either.

Tomorrow, Walks Alone knew, there would be no choice. Ghosts or not, she was going to have to return to the canyon for more water, more horse meat, a piece of fat, and, she hoped, a blanket that had been left behind. It would be another day, perhaps longer, before Gray In Hair was strong enough to travel. In the meantime, the girl had to eat and drink to make plenty of milk for her baby.

Gray In Hair spoke, her voice low. "My husband . . . he will be happy to see his daughter. I am grateful for what you have done."

Walks Alone swallowed hard. Gray In Hair had suffered enough. Now wasn't the time to tell her that her husband was one of the warriors Walks Alone had found dead in the canyon.

A soft breeze blew, ruffling the leaves on the surrounding bushes. Walks Alone closed her eyes. The memory of how her mother's gentle face had looked the last time she had seen her alive overwhelmed her and she fought to make it go away.

That scene was replaced by another. Little Hawk was kneeling by the pool in the canyon, drinking a handful of water and talking about the deer he hoped to kill for her.

Finally Walks Alone slept.

CHAPTER SIX

—◆—

CHUNKS OF HORSE MEAT and a couple of handfuls of unripe yucca fruit were roasting on the scraped-out coals of a small, smokeless campfire. Above the fire, more of the meat had been cut into long, thin strips and was hanging on a bent green mesquite limb. When the meat had dried into jerky, it could be carried for weeks, even months, without spoiling.

Walks Alone watched Gray In Hair. The new mother was sitting with her back against a boulder, rubbing her baby with a piece of meat fat. One Who Is Quiet was near the girl, trying to see how high he could stack a column of rocks before it fell.

A layer of thin clouds covered the noon sun, causing the day to be a little cooler than usual. Walks Alone sat down next to her brother. She was glad her trip back into the canyon was over. She had managed to find a blanket for the baby; she hoped it didn't belong to anyone who had been killed. Afterward she had filled the intestine canteen and hurriedly butchered more meat and a piece of fat from the fast-decaying dead horse.

There were hundreds of buzzards, crows, and ravens feeding on human carrion in the canyon, and she had seen two skulking coyotes. As before, she intended never to go back in the canyon again.

Walks Alone removed the buckskin wrap from her leg. Nearly all of the swelling was gone, but the skin around the wound was still purple and the burnt areas were sore.

Gray In Hair started to rise. "I did not know that you were hurt."

"No." Walks Alone waved a hand. "Do not get up. You should rest.

"When we were attacked by the soldier scouts a bullet struck my leg. It only went through a small amount of flesh in the back. Before I came to you I put hot embers on it. Today it is much better. It does not bother me to walk."

Gray In Hair lay back against the boulder. Her

daughter was asleep in her arms. She waved a fly off the child's ear.

"You went back into the canyon. Were many of our people killed in the fight?"

Walks Alone slipped the buckskin leg wrap through her belt, having decided the leg wound would heal faster in the open air. She was reluctant to answer Gray In Hair's question, yet the woman had to know.

She spoke slowly, keeping her eyes on Gray In Hair's face. "Many of the people were shot. Most were women and children. Victorio took the others and fled. My mother—she is gone. Your husband, he . . . he is also gone."

For a long moment Gray In Hair seemed not to hear. Then a single tear slid down the side of her nose. "Are you sure? Did you see his body?"

Walks Alone turned her head. The young woman's sorrow was causing her own emotions to stir, and she fought to control them.

"I saw."

Gray In Hair's hands started to shake. She set her baby on the blanket beside her and clutched her stomach, wailing softly and rocking back and forth.

Walks Alone picked up One Who Is Quiet and set him in her own lap. It was some time before Gray In Hair's cries waned and she grew still.

The girl looked up with a wet face. "I ask you to help me, Walks Alone. I ask you to help me and my baby go to my family's home at Mescalero. Will you do it?"

The request shocked Walks Alone. She turned away. When Gray In Hair was well enough, Walks Alone had planned to take her and follow Victorio's trail until they eventually rejoined the remaining band of Warm Springs Apaches. Also, once the band had arrived in a safe place and Victorio was able to spare one of his warriors, she believed there was a good chance that Little Hawk would start back over the trail to look for her and One Who Is Quiet.

But Mescalero? The Mescalero Indian reservation was several days' journey to the northeast.

Suddenly Walks Alone saw she had no choice. Apaches almost never called each other by name, but when they did, the matter was extremely serious. Gray In Hair had used Walks Alone's name and therefore her appeal could not be denied.

"I will do it," Walks Alone said. "We will need a horse to carry you, your daughter, and my brother. Today we will eat and rest. Tomorrow, before the sun, I will leave to try to get one."

CHAPTER SEVEN

THE SUN HADN'T been up long and already Walks Alone was thirsty. Knowing that Gray In Hair and One Who Is Quiet would need their water, she hadn't taken a drink from the intestine before leaving camp.

She jogged faster, forcing her mind off her thirst and the dull ache in her injured leg.

Five days before, while on their way to the canyon where they were attacked, Victorio and the band had skirted Hillsboro, a White Eyes' town. Walks Alone knew that Victorio sometimes raided the people there for much needed supplies. The town was sure to have horses, and Walks Alone could think of no closer place to find one. If she traveled fast enough, she should be able to reach the town sometime after dark.

A butterfly fluttered in front of Walks Alone, and without thinking she tried to grab it. The insect darted off and Walks Alone smiled, passing it by. When she was young, chasing butterflies had been one of her favorite pastimes. Her father had encouraged the activity, saying it would make her a better runner.

She had also liked to chase birds. Sometimes after a heavy rain she was able to catch them. Their wing feathers would be so wet they couldn't fly very fast.

More memories of childhood came to her mind. At Warm Springs she and other small girls had made dolls out of panic grass. They'd made beads for the dolls from ground cherries and wild-rose hips. Pine needles were used for bracelets and earrings.

The girls had built toy wickiups and tepees to resemble their own homes. Pillows, blankets, and beds for the dolls came from ferns. Leaves from various bushes and trees provided dresses, which were then decorated with side-oats grama grass. Food was gathered to put into the homes, with wild peas usually being the main dish.

When she grew older, Walks Alone had enjoyed

playing tag and hide-and-seek, and competing in footraces. She was a fast runner and was seldom beaten, even by the boys.

From the time Walks Alone was old enough to understand, her mother and grandmother had begun to teach her the things she would need to know to become an Apache wife and mother. She learned which plants were good for food and medicine, and how to gather, store, and prepare them. She sewed moccasins, wove baskets, tanned hides, made clothes, and cooked.

But there was another side to her training, a physical side she enjoyed and at which she excelled.

Almost every morning, even in winter, her mother or father made her swim. Afterward she was told to run to the top of a mountain and back down without stopping. Her father said the swimming and running would make her mind quick and strong, along with her body.

Two Horns also taught her how to identify tracks and how to follow them and sneak up on the animals that made them. He had only one gun, an old single-shot soldier's rifle that he had traded two horses and a quiver full of arrows for, but he made sure Walks Alone and her mother knew how to shoot it.

At Warm Springs, Walks Alone had spent

many late evenings with her father learning how to use a sling, throw a spear, and shoot a bow and arrow. She became fairly skillful in the use of all three. But her favorite training had been the riding of horses.

Both Snow On Her and Two Horns had been known throughout the tribe as skilled horse riders, and they had passed their knowledge and abilities on to their daughter. From the time Walks Alone was big enough to sit on a horse's back and clutch its mane without falling off, she had been riding.

As she grew older, her horsemanship training increased in level of difficulty. Riding bareback with only a rope around the horse's nose, she was told to race down steep mountainsides at full speed while leaning to the side and using one hand to pick up certain objects from the ground as she went. She had to jump her horse over logs, arroyos, boulders, and cactus. And she had to mount and dismount while at a run.

Once her father had given her a wild horse. It had taken her most of late spring, a time period known as Many Leaves, to tame the horse, but she had managed it without help from anyone.

Walks Alone had loved that horse. Loved him and the man who had given him to her too much. After her father's death, the horse had constantly reminded her of him. One day she took the animal to a distant mesa and set him free.

The hour had grown late. Walks Alone stepped lightly, feeling her way in the darkness. Somewhere ahead was water. She could tell by the musty smell of rotting vegetation and the sounds of crickets and frogs.

Less than a mile away were the lights of Hillsboro. She would go there if she had to, but earlier she had noticed the single lamp-lit window of what she guessed to be a ranch house. If there was a horse at the ranch, and that was likely, it would be quicker and easier to get than one in the town, where so many of the White Eyes were.

Walks Alone bent low, moving through a cluster of trees. A short while ago she had been so tired from her long day's journey it was all she could do to keep her legs moving. Now, however, apprehension gripped her, sharpening her senses and renewing her strength.

She stepped out of the trees and stopped. Directly in front of her was a large, sunken earthen tank filled with water. Beyond it, faintly visible in the starlight, were a broad, empty flat and the silhouette of a building. Though no light was coming from the structure, she was sure it was in the same spot where she had seen the light earlier. Whoever was inside must have gone to sleep.

The frogs and crickets were quiet a moment as Walks Alone crept to the edge of the water, lay on her stomach, and drank. Except for a few swallows of juice from a barrel cactus she had cut open at noon, this was the first liquid she'd had since last night.

After drinking, she washed her face and arms, then soaked her legs. Surprisingly, her injured leg didn't ache much worse than her other one. There was no hurry in going to the ranch. It would be wiser to wait and give whoever was there plenty of time to fall asleep.

The cool water felt good. Walks Alone thought about One Who Is Quiet, Gray In Hair, and the baby. They should be all right, as long as she was able to safely return to them. But what if she couldn't? What if something happened to her? The meat and water she had left with them wouldn't last long. Gray In Hair, nursing and carrying a new baby, wouldn't be able to travel far without help.

Walks Alone saw how cautious she needed to be. It wasn't only her life at stake now, but perhaps the lives of others.

Her thoughts turned to Victorio. The Apache scouts and the soldiers had followed his trail out of the canyon. They might have caught and attacked the small band of Warm Springs Apaches again. Little Hawk and her grandmother could be dead.

Walks Alone shrugged the frightening possibility away. The canyon fight was the first time she had ever known Victorio to be surprised. He would not let it happen again. Rather, he would wait until the time and terrain were right, position his warriors, and give the scouts and the soldiers a surprise of their own.

A horse whinnied from somewhere near the ranch house and Walks Alone's heart began to beat rapidly. She hadn't been wrong to come here. Hurriedly she slid back from the water, took her knife, and began cutting a strip of buckskin from the bottom edge of her dress. One cut completely around might be long enough to use for a bridle and reins, but she would cut two strips and tie them together to be sure. The buckskin wasn't as strong as a rope, but it would work so long as she didn't put too much pressure on the reins.

Finished, she looped the buckskin into a coil, slid it under her belt, and started around the tank toward the house. If the place was like other White Eyes' ranches she had seen, there would be a corral not too far from the house, and maybe another building where hay and saddles were kept.

Walks Alone's spirits rose. She remembered what her father had told her about the White Eyes. White people worked all the time, tearing up the land and building houses and corrals and fences. They plowed the ground and planted seeds and watered and hoed and harvested their crops. But the White Eyes really didn't own anything. Everything they had owned them. They were nothing but slaves to an ear of corn or a piece of pork fat.

The free life of the Apache was much better. No farms, ranches, or towns held them prisoner. Life Giver provided them with everything they needed. Even the Mexicans and the White Eyes were put on the land for a reason. Whatever these strange people had, made, or grew, it belonged to the Apaches, who were here first. And the Apaches were free to claim their property whenever they wished.

Walks Alone moved on in a crouch, making a wide circle around the house. Soon she could see the vague outline of another, smaller building, which she guessed to be the barn.

She sneaked closer, wishing that the area hadn't been cleared of timber. The grass had been grazed so short it was of little help in camouflaging her movements.

The horse whinnied a second time and Walks

Alone strained her eyes, finally able to make out the rails and posts of a corral.

A dog barked from near the house. Not the short, choppy bark of most dogs, but the excited, drawn-out bawl of a hunting dog. Walks Alone knew about hounds. White men had used them on the reservation at San Carlos to follow and tree bobcats and mountain lions. Once the big dogs were let loose on a scent trail, they rarely lost it.

More dogs howled, their shrill yelps sounding eager and hungry. Walks Alone took a step backward. Her chest felt so tight she could scarcely breathe.

Inside the house a lamp was lit and she heard a man shouting. She didn't understand the words, but she knew she was in trouble. The white man would have a gun.

She turned and started to run. The farther she went across the barren landscape, the more frightened she became, and the faster she pushed herself. The ache in her wounded leg grew more intense.

The hounds were still barking, their bawls getting closer instead of farther away. There could be just one reason. The dogs had caught her scent. She was the prey they were after.

A jagged stone snagged one of Walks Alone's feet, tripping her. She was going too fast to catch herself and she fell headlong, sprawling out on the ground.

The dogs were still coming. Walks Alone knew she couldn't possibly outrun them now. If she was caught out here in the open with only a knife with which to defend herself, the hounds would likely rip her to bits. Even if they didn't, they'd bark at her and hold her until the white man she'd heard shouting came and killed her.

Walks Alone pulled off her moccasins and hastened to her feet. She threw them as far as she could in the direction of the approaching dogs, then turned into a heated run that was every bit as rapid as before.

Maybe the dogs would stop and chew on the moccasins awhile. All she could think of to do was to try to get as far away from them as possible. Beyond that, she had no plan, no hope.

Throwing her moccasins didn't help. Walks Alone listened to the hounds above her heavy breathing. The dogs were getting closer with each running step she took.

She kept moving. Finally an idea came to her. Ahead a short distance she could see the surface of the water in the earthen tank glistening in the starlight. If she could get past the tank before the hounds caught her—get into the timber, where there were trees to climb and there was the possibility of jumping from one to another without leaving her scent on the ground—she *might* have a chance.

The dogs' baying was close and loud. Walks Alone glanced behind her. She could see them, a half dozen hounds or more, and they were almost upon her. With all the strength terror can produce, Walks Alone raced on.

Then something bumped against one of her legs. There was a low growl and she felt a tug on her dress. She was almost at the tank.

The dark shape of a large tree stood straight ahead of her. One of the dogs passed her, growling and nipping. She slammed into the trunk of the tree without slowing down, the force of it knocking the breath from her.

Frantically she climbed, the rough tree bark scratching and scraping her flesh.

A bolt of pain shot through her as one of the snarling, pouncing hounds clamped its sharp teeth on her right foot. The weight of the dog threatened to pull her down.

She gripped the tree tighter and kicked out with her free leg, smashing the side of the hound's head with her heel.

The dog let go and she climbed higher. She felt a thick branch and pulled herself over it, then found another and lifted her body so that she was standing on the first. The hounds below were frenzied, barking and jumping at the tree trunk.

Walks Alone fought to catch her breath. A giddy feeling came over her and for a moment she was certain she would fall. At last she caught a bit of air, then a little more.

She looked around her. There had to be another tree close enough that she could leap or swing to it.

There wasn't. The dogs had been too close. She hadn't had the time to choose a tree. The one she was in stood alone on the bank of the dirt tank. She could see the water below her.

Walks Alone tried to make herself think. She had to do something. In minutes the white man from the ranch would be here. He would have a gun and Walks Alone was certain he would use it.

Water. Hounds couldn't trail a scent in water. She knew this because the few times a bobcat or mountain lion had escaped from the hounds at San Carlos, it was because of a creek or river the animal had somehow managed to cross.

But the dogs below were watching her. They would see where she went.

With one hand, Walks Alone managed to put the coil of buckskin she'd cut for a bridle around her arm and unfasten her belt. She pulled her dress over her head and hung it from a small branch near her feet. Her moccasins hadn't done much to hold the hounds' attention. She could only hope that her dress would.

Walks Alone was naked, but that did not matter. To survive, to live one more hour, one more minute, was her only concern.

She tightened her belt around her, stuffing the buckskin coil beneath it. The dogs were jumping higher than ever, trying to reach her dress. She stepped farther out on the limb. For a brief moment she wondered how deep the water below was, then she bent her knees and dived.

The water splashed loudly. Walks Alone's hands touched the muddy bottom. She closed her eyes and began to move through the water.

A long time passed before Walks Alone's head broke the surface. Her lungs felt like they were on fire and it was hard to keep from coughing as she gulped in air.

The dogs were still barking. She couldn't see them, but it sounded like they were at the tree where she had left them.

Gently, so there would be no noise, she cupped her hands and continued to swim. At last she reached the far side, crawled up the muddy bank, and dropped in exhaustion. Nothing but sheer determination put her legs back under her and drove her on. There was no time to rest. The dogs could leave the tree at any moment.

The white man was sure to be following the sound of the dogs. He and perhaps others would show up soon. They would see her dress and they would take the hounds away from the tree and circle the tank with them, trying to pick up her scent again. If that happened, it was over. She knew she lacked the energy to run fast for very long again.

What she needed was the same thing she had come here for—a horse. There was a chance that no one was left at the ranch now and that the horse she'd heard was still there.

She stopped, indecision holding her. After a brief moment she concluded that going back to the ranch wasn't any riskier than heading for Hillsboro, and it might be her only hope. If the dogs followed her trail again, it wouldn't matter which direction she went—they'd get her. On top of a horse was the only way she could possibly escape them.

Walks Alone turned and started toward the light shining through one of the ranch house windows. This time she would not circle the place or exercise much caution. Either the horse was there and she would be able to mount it and leave, or this night promised to be her last.

A twinge of pain came from her right foot. She knew she had stepped on a cactus. The foot was already sore from the dog bite and she thought it might be bleeding. Her other leg still ached from the bullet wound.

She gritted her teeth, continuing on without missing a step. She was an Apache, and Apaches were trained from childhood to endure pain and hardship.

A different light several hundred yards off caught her eye. This one was bobbing up and down as if someone was carrying it. It was the white man, Walks Alone reasoned. He was carrying a lantern and going toward his dogs.

Walks Alone jogged faster. Since leaving the tank she hadn't been able to fully catch her breath, and it was becoming more and more difficult for her to take in enough air.

Soon the house was before her. She passed behind it without slowing down, aiming straight for the corral. Her heart beat violently as she climbed over the rail fence. There were two horses inside.

She edged slowly toward them, holding out her hand. The last thing she wanted to do was frighten them.

One of the horses, visible only as a dark shadow, snorted and shied away from her. The other remained still. Walks Alone let the horse smell her, then put her arm around its neck. She placed the center of the buckskin strip she'd cut into the horse's mouth and wrapped two half hitches around its nose. The two hanging strips left over were plenty long enough for reins.

Words were spoken. Walks Alone looked toward the house. It was the voice of a woman, yet she could see no one.

She found the gate, slid back the board latch, and shoved it open. The rusty hinges squeaked loudly. Far off, yet perhaps coming nearer, was the incessant bawling of the hounds.

The horse that she had startled followed the one that she led out the gate.

A scream came from the direction of the house. Walks Alone looked to see a figure rushing toward her with a long, slender object.

She grabbed the horse's mane and swung on, instantly gathering the reins, hissing, and digging her heels into the animal's sides. The horse took two bucking jumps, then leveled out into a dead run.

Behind her she could hear the second horse continuing to follow. She was glad. Unless there were other horses somewhere at the ranch, no one would be able to catch her.

CHAPTER EIGHT

✦◄══◆══►✦

WALKS ALONE pulled the bay mare to a stop, let the reins lie limp on the horse's neck, and rubbed her dry, tired eyes. The mare's colt, a sorrel stud almost as big as his mother, trotted alongside and lowered his head to snatch a tuft of grass.

Daylight was full now. Walks Alone looked down into the canyon she had just come from— the same canyon Victorio and his people had been camped in when they were attacked by the scouts.

Each time she had left the canyon and told herself she'd never return, necessity had drawn her back. Today was no different. After traveling throughout the night, she and the horses needed a drink. The stream in the canyon was the only water she knew of for miles.

And there was another reason for having to return. She needed something to wear.

Walks Alone had found a brown horse blanket near the trail her people had made fleeing. She didn't think that it belonged to any of the dead, and she felt extremely fortunate to have it. After unfolding the blanket, she discovered it was large enough so that all she had to do was make a slit in the middle and poke her head through.

A shadow flashed by on the ground and Walks Alone looked up. An eagle was flying high above. She watched the bird a moment, remembering one she had caught when she was young. She hadn't intended to catch it. The trap had been set for a rabbit. But when she checked the snare, an eagle was in it.

Because eagles and hawks fed on snakes, lizards, and other nasty things, no Apache would eat the large birds. Walks Alone tried to free the eagle, but it was too vicious. Her father had come and clubbed it. Since eagle feathers were always in great demand for use on arrows and for various rituals, he plucked the bird. Just when he'd finished, the featherless eagle came back to life. Unable to fly, it ran away.

Walks Alone nudged the mare forward. She wondered if that naked eagle had grown new feathers and was the one winging over her now.

Soon Walks Alone neared the campsite where she had left Gray In Hair and One Who Is Quiet. During the night she had stopped and pulled the cactus needles out of her foot, but it felt like a few were still there. The dog bite had turned out not to be too serious. The skin on top of her foot had been broken and it had bled some, but other than being bruised and sore, it would be all right.

The mare halted of her own accord, her ears rigid and pointed as if she had seen or heard something.

Walks Alone slid off the horse, standing close to its side. Something could be wrong, and a person on top of a horse made an easy target. The scouts might have found the campsite.

But it was Gray In Hair, holding her baby, who stepped out from behind a clump of bushes. She had cut her hair and it took a second look for Walks Alone to recognize her. One Who Is Quiet appeared and ran to Walks Alone, grabbing her leg.

She lifted the boy and set him on the mare, patting his shoulder. She turned to Gray In Hair.

"We have horses. No more will we have to walk."

"They are good ponies," Gray In Hair said. "They are strong and fat. We heard them coming and that is why we hid. Where did you get them?"

It took a while for Walks Alone to recount everything that had happened to her. At camp she lay on her back, chewing on a piece of jerky, while Gray In Hair examined the sole of her foot for more cactus needles.

Walks Alone was so weary she could hardly keep her eyes open, but she spoke. "When you are done, we will leave for Mescalero."

"You are not able to leave now," Gray In Hair scolded. "You rest. Tomorrow we will go."

"No." Walks Alone took her foot away, struggling to rise. "We will leave now. The White Eyes I took the horses from might be following the tracks. I do not want them to find us here."

Gray In Hair grabbed Walks Alone's foot and held it. "I am not finished. When I am, then we will go."

Breaking camp didn't take long, since they had nothing to take with them except the jerky and the small amount of water left in the intestine canteen.

Walks Alone held the baby while Gray In Hair mounted the mare. Then she handed the infant to her, picked up her brother, and swung him on behind.

She moved to the colt, which was standing close by, nibbling on a bush. She and Gray In Hair had coupled their belts together to make a bridle for him. The reins were too short, but the thick leather of the rawhide belt was stronger than the buckskin she had used to bridle the mare.

Walks Alone felt uneasy as she positioned the reins on either side of the colt's neck. She doubted if the young horse had ever been ridden before, and there was no telling what he might do.

Some horses she'd seen, when mounted for the first time, just stood in quiet bewilderment. Others bucked or became frightened and ran. A few reared. The rearing horse was the most dangerous. If the horse lost his balance and fell over backward, his weight would crush the rider.

Walks Alone knew that waiting to mount would only make her more nervous. Mescalero was a long way off and riding there would be much easier than walking.

She grabbed a handful of the horse's mane and swung on.

Nothing. The sorrel colt stood still. Walks Alone wondered if she had been wrong. Perhaps the horse had been ridden before.

She called to Gray In Hair, thinking that the colt might handle better if he was allowed to follow his mother as he had been doing.

"You go first."

Gray In Hair turned the mare and started off. Walks Alone nudged the colt with her heels. The colt took one hesitant step, then put his nose to the ground and bucked, throwing his hind legs high into the air. The move was quick and powerful. Walks Alone had no choice but to lean forward so she could keep her grip on the reins. She was out of balance, and for a moment she was sure she would tumble over the horse's head.

The colt's back feet hit the ground with bone-jarring solidness. He bucked again, this time pawing the air with his front feet. The force of the motion threw Walks Alone back behind the horse's withers, where she needed to be. She grabbed the mane with her free hand and braced herself for the jolt of the colt's landing.

The jolt didn't come. Out of the corner of her eye Walks Alone saw Gray In Hair and One Who Is Quiet race by on the mare. Instantly the colt broke into a run, doing his best to keep up with his mother.

Walks Alone relaxed a little. Compared to the bucking, the gallop was easy to ride. Ahead of her, Gray In Hair was holding her baby in one arm and the reins in the other. That the girl knew about horses was obvious. She had known that the colt needed something to get his mind off bucking, and by running the mare past him she had provided it.

Gray In Hair soon slowed the mare to a lope, then a trot. The colt now seemed preoccupied with just keeping up, and Walks Alone didn't try to use her heels or pull on the reins to guide him. It would be enough for the day if the young horse became accustomed to her weight and learned to accept it.

Hours passed, and the sun bore down hot. Walks Alone rode with her shoulders slumped and her eyes closed. Her head bobbed up and down with each step the colt took.

She wasn't all the way asleep, but nearly. She knew this was dangerous. She needed to be watching. The enemies of the Apache were many.

And then there was the colt. He could become frightened at most anything—a strangely shaped rock, a snake, or a mouse scurrying through a patch of dry weeds. He might buck or jump sideways and throw her off.

To sleep was foolish, but Walks Alone couldn't help it. For too long she had done too much. She was tired. Very tired.

CHAPTER NINE

———— ❖ ————

TWELVE DAYS had passed since the attack in the canyon. August now approached September, the season Apaches knew as Large Fruit.

Walks Alone sat in a grassy clearing midway up a steep ridge, resting her back against a tree stump. She felt better than she had in some time. For two days and nights she had been at Mescalero, doing nothing. Gray In Hair and her family hadn't allowed her to do anything but eat and sleep.

Below, in the valley, lay the Mescalero village—a haphazardly arranged cluster of brush wickiups, several skin-walled tepees, and a few white soldier tents. Campfire smoke rose above towering pines, and children were running and playing, looking like so many busy ants. Except for the tents, the peaceful village reminded Walks Alone of her home at Warm Springs before the White Eyes came.

She took her eyes off the village and looked at the ground. She knew she shouldn't spend time thinking about the dead, but she missed her mother—missed her terribly. And she missed her grandmother.

The only way she'd found to stop thinking about either of them was to think about Little Hawk, and that, too, made her sad. She wanted to see him, talk to him, and know that he was all right. The last thing he had told her before the scouts attacked was that he was going hunting and if he was successful, he wanted to give his kill to her. The statement showed he wanted to provide for her. It showed he was thinking of marriage.

The thud of hooves striking the ground broke into her thoughts, and Walks Alone glanced up to see the sorrel colt standing a few yards from her. She had ridden him up the mountain and then hobbled his front feet to allow him to graze. As soon as he cropped off the tall grama grass within reach of his nose, he would leap forward to fresh new grass. The horse still wasn't trained very well, but he was learning, and during the trip from the canyon to Mescalero she had become attached to him.

Their journey hadn't been easy. Both the mare and the colt had gone without water for more than two days before getting a small amount of muddy rainwater that had collected in the ruts of an old wagon road. Grass, too, was scarce in places, and by the time the horses reached the reservation their flanks were badly drawn.

The horses weren't the only ones that suffered on the four-day trip. If it hadn't been for the juice of an occasional barrel cactus and the few swallows of water they had obtained from the basal leaves of a mescal plant, Walks Alone wasn't sure Gray In Hair and her nursing baby would have made it.

Food shouldn't have been a problem, but it was. Their first night out a coyote had entered their camp and got away with their jerky. Having nothing else, and not wanting to take time to hunt for rats, rabbits, or sparrows, they ate what yucca, screwbean, and prickly pear cactus they came across. There hadn't been much, and what they had come across often wasn't ripe, but it had sustained them.

Walks Alone leaned her head back. She was glad the trip was over, happy that Gray In Hair was united with her people. But she didn't plan to stay here at Mescalero long. Just long enough for the colt and mare to fatten, and for Walks Alone to make a pair of moccasins and a bow and set of arrows for herself and One Who Is Quiet. Her people, her grandmother, and Little Hawk were somewhere. She had to find them.

Walks Alone turned to see Gray In Hair approach.

"Where is your baby?" she asked.

"She is with her grandmother. I fed her and waited for her to sleep. Then I followed your pony's tracks. That is how I found you."

"Is my brother also with your mother?"

"Yes. He is fine."

Walks Alone gestured for Gray In Hair to sit beside her. "Why have you come?"

After Gray In Hair was seated she answered. "You know that today there will be a big feast. A young girl has become a woman. You are my friend. I do not want you to stay up here on this mountain by yourself. I want you to go down to the feast with me."

Walks Alone shook her head. "I cannot. I am in mourning."

Gray In Hair rose up on her knees. "Look at my dress. Do you see that it is old and worn? It does not look any better than the blanket that covers you. We are both in mourning. It will be many

70

new moons before either of us will wear good clothes.

"But to go to the feast is not wrong. Everyone should be there. We should wish this girl a long and good life, a good family, and many good child-bearing years. In this way, no matter how many of us are killed, there will always be Apaches."

Walks Alone stared blankly at the valley below. Her thoughts were on her own coming-of-age ceremony. For eight days and nights she had been White Painted Woman. The rite had been one of the most important events of her life and all of the people at Warm Springs had supported her by celebrating her entrance to womanhood.

"You are right," Walks Alone said, getting to her feet. "We should go to the feast to honor this girl. I will take my brother. Perhaps White Painted Woman will choose to give the people a blessing."

A short while later, at noon, Walks Alone sat with her legs folded beneath her, chewing on a piece of boiled venison. Beside her, One Who Is Quiet was using his fingers to eat the mescal that had been heaped onto a piece of plate-shaped rawhide.

The Mescalero people were gathered around a large open area near the southern end of the village. Everyone was in high spirits, eating, talking, and laughing while anxiously awaiting the appearance of White Painted Woman.

Gray In Hair was seated in front of Walks Alone, holding her baby. She stood, pointing to the south.

"I see White Painted Woman. She is coming."

In moments all of the people were standing. Walks Alone set One Who Is Quiet on her shoulders so he could see better. The Mescalero girl, who for the days of her ceremony would be referred to only as White Painted Woman, was walking slowly, following her attendant.

The sight of the girl's ceremonial dress reminded Walks Alone of the dress her mother and grandmother had made for her.

Her own dress had been fashioned out of five doeskins and decorated with circles that represented the sun. The long fringes on the sleeves and bottom were symbolic of sunbeams. The morning star and crescent moon were stitched on the front, as well as connecting arcs that stood for rainbows.

An elderly woman had blessed the dress by singing over it for weeks as it was being made. Another woman, also aged, had been Walks Alone's attendant during the rite and provided her with instruction.

For the four days of the ceremony, and for four days after it, Walks Alone had done all of her drinking through a *carrizo* tube suspended from her dress. Her lips could not touch water. If they did, a heavy rain would come and ruin the feast.

As Walks Alone continued to watch the Mescalero girl, other rules she had had to follow came to mind. If she needed to scratch, it had to be done with the branch of a fruit or nut-bearing tree. Using her fingernails would have caused scars that would remain for life. She was not allowed to eat much or leave her tepee except when told to do so. She had to be careful not to talk much or laugh. Laughter would have caused her face to become old and wrinkled before her time.

Walks Alone's mother had told her that during the time she was White Painted Woman, she must have a good disposition and do everything she was told without grumbling. If she cursed or became angry, she would be a mean and hated woman for the rest of her life. If she was pleasant and cheerful, her mother said, she would always be that way and everyone would love her.

The Mescalero girl and her attendant stopped near the opening of a tepee-shaped structure made of four tall spruce poles and sided with oak boughs. This was the symbolic home of White Painted Woman. The girl lay down on a buckskin with her head to the east and her attendant began to rub her body, working from her head to her feet and from her right side to her left. This would mold the girl, making her strong, straight, and healthy.

Soon a group of singers appeared, and while the girl danced, songs were sung about the blessings White Painted Woman had bestowed on the people.

The songs also told the story of creation. Hundreds of harvests ago, there was the creator, Life Giver. There was also White Painted Woman. She gave birth to many babies who were eaten by the Owl Giant.

Then White Painted Woman was made pregnant by Water. Four days later, Child of Water was born. Because the Owl Giant had eaten most of her other children, White Painted Woman was worried that he would eat her new son too. So the wise woman dug a hole under her campfire and hid the infant there, where he would be warm. She took him out of the hole only to feed and wash him.

Soon Child of Water could walk. One day the Owl Giant came to White Painted Woman and noticed tiny footprints on the ground. The giant was filled with fury and wanted to know where the child was who had made the tracks. White Painted Woman told him that she herself had made them.

She had made them because she missed her other children.

The Owl Giant did not believe her, so White Painted Woman made more tracks on the ground that were exactly like the ones that were there. This helped convince the giant that she was telling the truth, and after a time he left.

Child of Water lived to become a man. He killed all of the evil creatures in the world: the giant eagles, the buffalo bulls, and the antelope that could kill their victims with a glance. He was even able to defeat the Owl Giant. Later he forced all of those he conquered to agree to become useful to man.

It was Child of Water and White Painted Woman who had given the people instructions on how to perform the coming-of-age ceremony.

The singing stopped and Walks Alone, weary of the weight of her brother, set him down. The Mescalero girl knelt on the buckskin and rocked back and forth, imitating the posture of White Painted Woman. Presently she rose, and a medicine man blessed her by putting corn kernels on her head to assure that she would always have food.

The girl danced a second time, and threw the buckskin she had been using to the east to show that there would always be meat on the fire and good hunting for everyone. Blankets were brought to her, and she threw them to the four directions to ensure that she would always have warmth and that her camp would always be clean. Then she left the grounds in the same manner she had entered.

Walks Alone sighed, glancing down at her brother, who was eating more of the mescal. She knew the day's ceremony was not over. There would be social dancing, and this evening masked dancers would appear to drive away evil spirits.

But she did not want to stay any longer. While the ceremony had reminded her of happier days at Warm Springs, it had also reminded her of what she had lost.

Right now, more than anything, she wanted to see Little Hawk.

CHAPTER TEN

ONE WHO IS QUIET notched an arrow in the string of his new bow, his face beaming. He pulled the arrow back, aimed at the horizon, and released. The arrow flew in a high arc halfway across the meadow before landing in the tall grass.

Walks Alone grinned as her brother hurried off to find the arrow. She had made him two more arrows, but until he learned to shoot well, he would be given only one. That is how her father had taught her to shoot. With just one arrow, the archer had to pay attention to accuracy. There would be no second chance if the target was missed.

As Walks Alone continued to watch her brother, she resolved to start spending more time with him, teaching him those things she could. Because the band of Warm Springs Apaches had been constantly on the move, One Who Is Quiet's physical training had been neglected. She knew he needed to learn to hunt with a sling, a spear, and a bow, and to distinguish between the various animal tracks. He should be learning more about horses—how to care for them, bridle them, and ride them. And he must know how to use a fire drill, how to cook, and how to make smoke when he wished to signal someone.

The boy needed to be swimming and running every day, and it was time he started participating in supervised wrestling matches with other boys his age.

What One Who Is Quiet needed most, Walks Alone realized, was a father.

Little Hawk came to her mind. The young warrior was kind, soft-spoken, and patient. He would make a good father for her brother, or at least a good friend.

One Who Is Quiet jumped high and waved the arrow, showing he'd found it. He began to run back toward his sister.

Walks Alone took her own bow from her shoulder and examined it. Like her brother's, it had been made from the split branch of a mulberry tree. To make the curve, she'd bent the bow over her knee, tied it tightly, and placed it in hot ashes, being careful not to let it burn. When the wood cooled it held its shape. She had made a bowstring from the sinew of a deer one of the Mescalero men had brought to camp.

She ran her fingers along the edge of the wood. While the bow was usable, it needed to be stronger. She wanted to cover it with a glue she'd make by boiling the hooves and horns of animals, and then wrap the length of it with sinew. That was how her father had made his bow, and it was one of the strongest she'd ever seen.

But first she would make more arrows. It had been just a week since the Mescalero girl's coming-of-age ceremony had ended, and making arrows was slow work. Warriors sometimes spent more than a month making a single bow and a quiver full of arrows.

One Who Is Quiet rushed up to his sister and notched his arrow in the bowstring, signaling that he wanted to shoot again. Walks Alone smiled and nodded. She hadn't seen her brother so happy since before their mother had died.

The boy's arrow was in the air when a movement to the side caught Walks Alone's attention. She watched as Gray In Hair, holding her baby and taking long, quick steps, emerged from a thick stand of aspen trees.

"I am glad I have found you," Gray In Hair called. As she drew closer, she continued to speak. "The men are gathered with the leaders of the tribe. The chief has requested our presence at the council. He is there waiting for us."

Walks Alone frowned. Women were almost never invited or permitted to attend a council of the warriors. There had to be a serious reason for this summons.

"Are we the only women who were asked to come?"

"Yes. I think that is so." Gray In Hair opened the blanket more around her baby's face. She looked out at the meadow, where One Who Is Quiet was searching for his arrow.

"My mother will care for your brother and my daughter. Come. We must hurry."

The council was being held in a large open area near the southern end of the village. Walks Alone guessed that there were at least eighty or ninety warriors crowded around a small central circle of men who were seated on the ground.

These men were the leaders, respected for their age, wisdom, speechmaking, or fighting abilities. They were influential men, yet they, like their chief, did not have absolute power. The people followed them only as long as what the men did agreed with them. Otherwise, new leaders would eventually be recognized, or those who were dissatisfied would simply gather their belongings and move to another location.

A path opened among the standing warriors. Walks Alone's heart beat hard as she followed Gray In Hair to the center circle. There a heavily wrinkled man with long white hair and a dark, broad face motioned for them to sit in a bare spot across from him. Walks Alone had seen the man at the coming-of-age ceremony and knew that he was the chief of the Mescaleros.

She and Gray In Hair had hardly been seated before the man stood. Despite his many years and frail-looking body, his deep voice was lively and clear.

"You are all here." The chief spread out his arms and let them drop to his side. "I will tell you the reason for this council. Victorio, Chief of the Warm Springs Apaches, is making trouble. He and his braves are raiding and killing the whites and the Mexicans wherever they go. The soldiers here think we are helping him. They think we are giving him supplies and fresh horses. They think some of our young men have fled the reservation and are with him."

He swept a few strands of loose hair from his face, then continued, his voice gruffer and louder than before.

"Because of the trouble Victorio is causing, the Indian agent and the soldiers want all Mescaleros to go to the Agency. There they will take our weapons and our horses, and they will keep them until Victorio is captured or killed. We will not be able to hunt. We will have nothing to hunt with. Our families will go hungry. Victorio is the cause of this. He is the one who is to blame."

Walks Alone knew better—knew she shouldn't speak unless asked to—but her feelings about the chief's attack on her people and her leader were strong. She started to rise.

Gray In Hair caught her arm, holding her down. As she did, another man, also aged, stood and began to speak.

"Your words, my chief, are not true. Victorio is not to blame. He is doing only what other great leaders of our people have done. Mangas Coloradas, Juh, Cochise, Geronimo, Naiche, Loco, and others fought the White Eyes for their freedom and for their land.

"We are the ones to be blamed and pitied. We have quit fighting. We are afraid of the whites. Their numbers have no end and their guns do not run out of bullets. So we live on land within boundaries that hold us like so many dogs on a chain."

The elderly man paused, taking a deep breath. "Victorio is not to blame for what the whites do to us. He is to be honored for his courage and for what he is doing to them."

Several warriors yelled out their agreement. The Mescalero chief raised his hands with the palms out until the men were quiet.

"You all know me," the chief said. "You know that I have fought the White Eyes plenty. I fought until all of my family was gone. I fought until the pain and hunger cries of our women and children were so loud I could hear nothing else. And the White Eyes still kept coming.

"We must live in peace with the whites. Cochise could not win against them. Mangas Coloradas could not win against them. Victorio will not win against them either. He will succeed only in making his people suffer. If he does not quit fighting, not one of those who follow him now will be left."

For a long moment the chief was silent. Then he set his gaze on Walks Alone and Gray In Hair. "You were both with Victorio. Tell us what he will do. Will he continue to fight, or will he surrender?"

Gray In Hair looked at Walks Alone, indicating with her eyes and a lift of her chin that she wanted her to answer.

Walks Alone nervously rose to her feet. "I—" She cleared her throat, knowing her voice needed to be louder. "I can only tell you what I think. Unless the White Eyes allow Victorio and the people to return to our home at Warm Springs, he will keep fighting. The White Eyes have lied to him too many times. He does not trust them. He will not surrender to them."

She stopped, hesitant to say more because she was a woman and she knew that the warriors would quickly tire of her.

The chief nodded, and she continued. "I have heard the words that have been spoken. It is true that the Mescaleros are caged on a reservation. But your reservation is in the heart of your homeland. You have your valleys and trees. You have your hunting grounds and your sacred mountain. Victorio and those with him have nothing."

Walks Alone lowered her head and sat down. She was short of breath and not able to fully remember what she had just said. She anxiously awaited the chief's reaction.

The man remained still a long moment before turning from her.

"Listen to me. All of you. We must go to the Agency tomorrow. The soldier chief has said he will hunt down every one of us who does not go. Our homes are here. Our game and our mountains are here. To fight the White Eyes would cause sorrow and suffering. Nothing more would be gained."

The chief looked at the older man who had talked earlier, then at Walks Alone.

"No more do I blame Victorio. He is fighting because he must. That is all. I have spoken."

CHAPTER ELEVEN

❦

FOR THREE DAYS and nights it had been raining.
It had been raining ever since the Mescaleros
had reported to the Indian Agency and were
placed in a manure-filled corral.

Walks Alone peered out between the corral
rails at the soldiers who guarded them. She wished
she and her brother had not come with the
Mescaleros to the Agency. She wouldn't have, except she didn't think it was yet time to leave the
reservation and begin her search for her people.
The mare and colt still needed to gain a little more
weight, and she wanted to make a pair of moccasins for herself and finish her bow. She also

needed to make more arrows and braid a length of rope and two strong bridles for the horses.

If she had only known what the Indian agent and the soldiers were planning to do. All of the Indians thought they were just going to report to the Agency for a head count, give up any horses or weapons they hadn't hidden before coming, and return to their homes. Instead they were seized and thrown inside the large, open corral, with no blankets, no firewood, and very little food.

Walks Alone looked down into her lap at One Who Is Quiet. His eyes were closed and his skin pale. He had gotten sick the first night they'd spent in the wet corral. Now he was worse. Much worse.

The boy wasn't the only one who was ill. There were others. It seemed the young and the old were suffering the most.

She leaned her upper body as far as she could over One Who Is Quiet, trying to shield him from the rain. When darkness fell, she'd do what she should and would have done already, had she known how long the White Eyes were going to hold them.

She would try to escape. Try to get blankets and find the eagle's feather, the bag of pollen, and the piece of turquoise a shaman had told her were in his tepee. If she brought these items to the shaman, the ceremony would be performed and One Who Is Quiet would be healed.

Clouds hid the stars. The night was black. The soldiers had placed lanterns along the corral's perimeter so they could watch their prisoners from comfortable positions beside warm campfires.

Walks Alone inched her way toward a corner of the corral that wasn't quite as closely guarded or as well lit as the rest of it. She had left One Who Is Quiet with Gray In Hair. The boy wasn't any better. If anything, his gasps for breath were more difficult.

One of two soldiers nearest Walks Alone reached for a coffeepot hanging above their fire. The other soldier turned too, picking up his cup.

Walks Alone slid under the bottom fence rail. At once she was up and running.

Shouts sounded behind her. The report of a gun was loud, echoing against the hills. In moments she was rushing blindly through darkness. She forced herself to slow. The danger of running into a tree or falling into a gorge or hole was greater than that of the soldiers who were undoubtedly chasing her.

Still, Walks Alone continued to travel as fast as

she dared. She wondered if she should have waited until later in the night, when the soldiers would be sleepy, to attempt her escape. Perhaps if she had, she wouldn't have been noticed. But One Who Is Quiet was too ill. Another long night without the warmth of a blanket might be more than he could stand.

Presently she stopped to rest and listen. The rain that had earlier been only a drizzle was falling heavily.

For now she believed she was safe. No one could possibly find her until daylight, and she planned to be back inside the corral with her brother long before then.

Walks Alone knew the Mescalero chief would be displeased with her for leaving the corral. Many of the warriors had wanted to escape too, but the chief had repeatedly argued against it, saying that everyone would soon be released. She had believed that too, for a while.

Anger stirred in Walks Alone against the soldiers and Indian agent who had imprisoned them. All of her life the White Eyes had been her and her people's enemies. But even the death of her mother at the hands of paid army scouts hadn't caused her to hate the White Eyes like she did now. White men treated dogs, pigs, and horses better than they did Indians. They should have to pay for what they were doing. They too should be made to suffer.

A bolt of lightning cut across the sky, followed by an earsplitting roar. The noise was the voice of the Thunder People, Walks Alone knew. And the lightning strike was one of their arrows.

She started to run. Whenever the Thunder People who lived in the clouds were aroused or angered, they sprayed arrows everywhere, especially at those they wished to punish. She hoped their aim was for the soldiers stationed around the corral, and not for any of the people who were in it.

Walks Alone knelt behind a small thicket of oak brush, watching the corral and the soldiers on guard. She had been to the village and gotten all the blankets she could carry. And she'd been fortunate to find the items the shaman had requested in order to perform the healing ceremony for her brother.

It was still early in the night. She reasoned that waiting until later to slip unseen into the corral would be the wisest. But One Who Is Quiet's illness could not wait. He needed the healing ceremony performed for him immediately. And he needed the warmth of the blankets.

Walks Alone rose up some so she could see better. The rain continued to pour down and the soldiers were staying close to their campfires, trying to keep them ablaze. They wouldn't be watching for her. They would never guess that she would return.

A few of the soldiers at one end of the corral started laughing. Walks Alone took a deep breath, stepped around the oak brush, and sprinted for the corral fence.

Someone shouted, the man's deep, booming voice so close it startled Walks Alone and caused her to stumble. She turned her head to see a bearded soldier not more than a body's length from her drop the firewood in his arms and rush toward her.

Terror gripped her. She leaped in a desperate attempt to reach the corral fence. The soldier caught the back of the blanket that covered her. She was falling. She threw the bundle of blankets up, saw them fly over the fence.

Then she was down, her face plowing thick mud. The soldier who had her dropped heavily on top of her. He scrambled to his feet, yanking her up with him by the short hair on her head. He put an arm around her waist and held her tightly.

Other soldiers quickly crowded around. Laughing, jeering soldiers. The arm around her waist dropped and she kicked out, trying to break free.

One blow struck her stomach, another her side. A soldier slapped her and she spit at him. He wiped his face with his coat sleeve, took a step back, and swung, his fist hitting her full in the face with a sharp clap.

Walks Alone was dizzy. She couldn't see. Again and again the soldiers hit her. Finally, yelling and cheering, they raised her over their heads and threw her into the corral.

As she lay on the ground, every part of Walks Alone hurt.

Hands touched her and she heard the voices of Apaches.

She spoke, her speech barely above a whisper "The bag . . . It is on my belt. The turquoise . . . the eagle's feather . . . the pollen are inside it. My brother . . . the ceremony. He . . . he must have it."

A man spoke. Walks Alone thought the voice was that of the Mescalero chief.

"Be still. Do not talk. Your brother no longer needs a ceremony. He is gone from here. He is no more."

CHAPTER TWELVE

WALKS ALONE slid wearily from the sorrel colt. All around her lay an expanse of parched, barren desert with only a narrow ribbon of green winding through the middle of it.

The green was the vegetation along the banks of the Rio Grande. The last time she saw the river had been with Victorio and the band, on their way to a hiding place in Mexico's Candelaria Mountains. That had been a harvest, possibly two harvests, ago.

She slid the strap holding the crude rawhide canteen she'd made off of her shoulder and drank the two remaining swallows of water. If she continued to ride steadily, she would reach the Rio

Grande before dark. There she'd have all the water she wanted. And once she crossed the river, she'd be in Mexico. Two more days of riding would put her into the mountains where she hoped to find Victorio and her people.

The sadness that had filled Walks Alone since her brother's death, nearly a new moon ago, grew heavier. It would be difficult to face her grandmother and Little Hawk and tell them that because of her foolishness, One Who Is Quiet was gone.

Again, as she had done many times before, Walks Alone ran the events leading up to her brother's death through her mind. If only she had been wise enough not to report to the Agency with the Mescaleros, they would both probably be sitting beside a fire with their grandmother by now. Additional arrows, stronger bridles, moccasins, and fatter horses were stupid reasons for having stayed. It had all been a mistake. A horrible mistake.

Walks Alone continued to gaze into the distance. She should have tried to escape from the corral the first night One Who Is Quiet became sick. If she had gotten the supplies then, the warmth of the blankets and a healing ceremony performed by the shaman would surely have made him well.

Her vision blurred from the mist in her eyes. The day after her brother died everyone in the corral had been released. Although she was badly hurt from the beating she'd taken, with at least one broken rib and a broken nose, she and Gray In Hair had tried to get One Who Is Quiet's body from the Indian agent so they could bury it properly. But the agent had told them that the soldiers had already buried the body, and he refused to tell them where the grave was.

Later, when Walks Alone was well enough, she'd returned to the place where she and One Who Is Quiet had hidden their bows and arrows before going to the agency. There she'd made a fire and burned them so that nothing, not even her own bow, would remain to remind her of him.

Four days ago Walks Alone had risen early, before the morning star appeared, and rode out of the village. She'd left the mare tied near Gray In Hair's wickiup but hadn't woken her to tell her about the gift. She knew that her friend would have tried to stop her from leaving until she was completely healed, and Walks Alone did not want to hear her arguments.

Her mind was made up. The Mescalero village held nothing for her. And as long as she moved carefully, the pain in her side wasn't too bad. As for her nose, no matter where she was, nothing but time was going to heal it.

The big colt began to walk faster, soon moving into a trot. The horse smelled the water ahead and he was thirsty.

Walks Alone glanced up at the setting autumn sun, then at the hedge of salt cedar trees lining the Rio Grande in front of her. There would be plenty of daylight left in which to drink and wash. More than anything else, she wanted to soak her body in the cool water.

Especially her face. Even though her nose wasn't nearly as swollen and discolored as it had been, it was awfully sore, and the last few days of constant wind and sun exposure hadn't helped it.

She heard the neigh of a horse, the nearness of it alarming. Walks Alone jerked her head to see two horses standing side by side a hard stone's throw to her right. On the saddled horses were two men, their faces hidden by wide-brimmed sombreros.

Walks Alone stared at them, numbed and confused. How could she possibly have missed the riders until now? She'd been warily scanning the terrain for hours. Everyone was the enemy of the Apache, and the last thing she wanted was for anyone to be able to get this close to her.

The river, she reasoned. The men had to have been by the river and hidden from view by the trees.

The colt paid no attention to the horses, his pace quickening the closer he came to the water. Walks Alone tried to appear calm, making herself look straight ahead while watching the men from the corner of her eye. That they were Mexicans, there was no doubt. Hopefully they were just a couple of vaqueros searching for lost cattle, and whatever interest they had in her would pass.

The riders suddenly spurred their horses and charged toward her. Walks Alone dug her bare heels into the colt's sides and hissed, urging him into a gallop.

She glanced behind. The rider closest to her had a lasso in his hand; the other had a pistol. Her scant lead on them was fast diminishing.

Why? Walks Alone almost shouted the word. Instantly she believed she had the answer. The colt was the only thing she had, so the men must be after him.

Then a sickening thought struck her. She did have something else, something that was probably more valuable than the horse.

Her scalp.

Many times she'd heard stories about Apaches who had fallen victim to professional scalp hunters.

The Mexican government paid the hunters for the scalps, and the price received for the hair of women and children was the same as it was for that of warriors.

The colt continued to run, and Walks Alone ducked low when he crashed through the line of salt cedars and splashed into the river. The water was murky and shallow and he slid to a stop in the mud, lowering his head to drink.

Walks Alone kicked furiously trying to drive him on. It was no use. He was too thirsty.

The two Mexicans broke through the trees, their horses' hooves hitting the water and spraying it everywhere. Frightened by the action and noise, the colt lunged forward into the deep river channel. At the same time, the rider holding the rope threw his loop.

Walks Alone saw it coming. She slid off the colt into the river, still tightly grasping his mane. The loop barely missed her, settling on the horse's back, then harmlessly slipping over his rump and into the water.

The Mexicans yelled angry words Walks Alone did not understand. The one with the pistol raised it and fired. The gun belched smoke and roared twice more before both riders jumped their mounts into the main channel after her.

Walks Alone stayed in the water, exposing only

her head and continuing to hold on to the colt's mane. Getting back on the horse would hinder his ability to swim and make her an easier target.

She watched the two riders behind her, watched their horses swim. The only hope she had was that the colt would outdistance them once he reached the bank.

Her hope quickly vanished, vanished like the blood she saw seeping into the swirling water. The colt was hurt. One or more of the Mexicans' gunshots had hit him. She couldn't tell where.

A bullet splattered the water a hand's length from Walks Alone's head. She pushed her face into the colt's damp neck and tried to gain control of her thoughts.

The colt was bleeding heavily. Even if he reached the other side of the river, there was no way he would be able to carry her for long. And if the scalp hunters caught her on foot out in the open, they'd quickly ride her down.

Then an idea came to Walks Alone. A risky notion that she hated yet believed to be her only chance. She would allow the man with the pistol to have a better view of her. When he shot again, she would act like the bullet hit her whether it did or not. She'd hold her head and scream, then dive deep into the water, fighting to swim against the swift current.

If she could stay under long enough for the riders to pass her, she'd attempt to swim to the bank. The scalp hunters would think she was either dead or wounded, and they'd search for her downstream. They would not guess that she was behind them.

Walks Alone inched her head away from the colt. She understood that the odds of the purposely drawn gunshot hitting her were greater than those of it missing. But she had to do something. To remain as she was proffered no hope. No chance.

The rider with the pistol saw her and began to take aim. She pushed herself out a little farther from the colt.

Without warning a strange force began to pull at Walks Alone's legs and hips. It became harder and harder for her to keep her grip on the colt's mane.

She glanced from the Mexican riders to the water swirling around her in a furious spray of white foam. A whirlpool encircled her. Such pools could be treacherous. It was the Water Monster who caused whirlpools. The monster was responsible whenever anyone or anything disappeared in the water. Sometimes grown men and even horses and cattle were pulled beneath without ever surfacing again.

All at once the power of the current ripped Walks Alone's hands from the colt's mane. She heard the muffled crack of a gunshot and water gushed over head, filling her ears.

She was spinning now, sinking, going down deeper and deeper. She kicked and tried to swim free. Her efforts were futile. Like a leaf in a strong wind, she was tossed and spun end over end.

The raging water was dark around her. Walks Alone's lungs felt like they would burst. Her head pounded and all sense of balance and direction was lost. She did not know up from down.

She continued to struggle but the churning undertow was too powerful. Her arms and legs began to tingle, then fell limp. A strange, peaceful feeling came over her and she felt as if she would sleep.

Suddenly the center of the current slammed her into a tangled mass of submerged branches that clawed at her blanket and skin. Alert now, she managed to lock her legs around one of the branches.

Just when she could stand no more—when even the will to live was all but gone—the water calmed. She released her hold on the branch and her body quickly floated to the surface.

Walks Alone was nearly dead. Her mouth was open and she was swallowing air as fast as her lungs could take it in, but she had no knowledge of it.

She vomited. Slowly her awareness began to return, and the clouds blocking her vision faded. Her mind started to work in bits and pieces. *The loop of a rope; a pistol; blood in the water.*

Then it all returned to her and she jerked upright in the water. Her feet touched the muddy bottom and she saw that she was close to the bank on the Mexican side of the river.

The air she had so badly needed continued to revive her. She looked down the river. The two scalp hunters were far enough away that they appeared small. She could see no sign of the colt.

Walks Alone moved to the bank, barely able to squirm over it. The Water Monster's whirlpool had helped her escape. Perhaps Life Giver had ordered the Monster to pull her under so that she would be saved from a bullet. But the Monster had held her too long. He had almost killed her himself.

Still panting for breath, Walks Alone crawled to the cover of the salt cedar trees. She pulled herself to her feet, shaking and faint.

Again she looked into the distance at the scalp hunters, knowing that they could leave the channel at any time and ride back up along the riverbank.

Resolve filled her, giving her strength. She took a step, then another. She must not let them find her.

CHAPTER THIRTEEN

WALKS ALONE woke to the hollow sound of a horse's unshod hooves striking solid ground. Before her eyes were fully open she reached for her knife and rolled to the side, coming up on her feet in a low crouch. The action caused pain to shoot from her sore muscles and ribs.

A spotted gray horse stood in front of her. She looked up at its rider, unable to see him clearly in the glare of the late-morning sun.

Walks Alone shielded her eyes with her free hand and the tension in her eased. The man was an Indian, an Apache she knew. Round Nose, the warrior her grandmother had wanted her to marry, stared blankly down at her.

The brave's bare chest was marked by numerous battle scars. He spoke. "I was hunting and Crow led me here. It is good that I have found you. The people think that you are gone."

Walks Alone stood, sheathing her knife. She scanned the desert, her eyes resting on the hazy blue Candelaria Mountains, a long day's ride to the south. Considering her physical condition, she had traveled far during the night. Her fear of the scalp hunters had driven her. She hadn't stopped until she had stumbled and dropped. And then she'd made several attempts to rise before finally giving up and falling asleep.

She glanced back at Round Nose, then pointed at the mountains. "Are our people there? Is my grandmother there? Is—" She caught herself, knowing it might not be wise to mention Little Hawk's name to the warrior.

The man gestured at the emptiness to the east of the Candelarias. "Victorio and everyone are there. They are moving on their way to the lakes of Tres Castillos. There, Victorio has said, the people will rest and make raids on the Mexicans for much needed supplies."

The warrior reached behind him, patting the horse's back. "It is better to ride than to walk. I have found you. I will take you to your grandmother."

Walks Alone grabbed the crook of his arm and swung on behind him, wincing from the pain the move caused her. She leaned back and breathed deeply. She was hungry and thirsty, bruised and sore, but it didn't matter. Soon she would see her grandmother.

They rode in silence. Walks Alone knew that Round Nose could not have helped but notice her broken nose and the absence of her brother. The brave undoubtedly had many questions. But he would wait for the answers. Patience in such matters was the way of the Apache. Others were also sure to have questions and there was no need for her to have to tell her story more than once.

A while later Round Nose halted the spotted pony. Not far ahead, traveling in a long dusty line, was the band of Warm Springs Apaches. A smile spread across Walks Alone's face.

It had been only two new moons since she had been with her people, yet it seemed at least two harvests.

Round Nose motioned to his right at a lone brave riding a pinto across a distant swell. "There is one here who did not think that you were gone. He spent many days going back to look for you. You belong with him. You should go to Little Hawk."

During their ride Walks Alone had been careful not to touch Round Nose any more than was necessary. She hadn't wanted to give him any no-tion that she might be interested in him. Now, however, she hugged him, laying the side of her face against his back.

He held his arm out for her and she grabbed it, swinging down lightly.

Then she started to run in the direction of the pinto.

It wasn't long before the mounted warrior was racing toward her. Drawing close, Little Hawk slid his horse to a dusty stop and jumped off.

He threw his arms around Walks Alone, lifting her up and swinging her around. The action hurt her, but she didn't let it show.

"I knew I would see you again," Little Hawk said, setting her down.

She pushed away from him, wiping tears of joy from her eyes while looking around to see if any-one was watching. The people would not approve of this open display of affection.

She took his hands in hers. Somehow he looked taller and stronger than she remembered.

"Life Giver has helped me," she said. "I have much to tell everyone. But now I will go to my grandmother."

Little Hawk released her hands and gently touched her battered face with the tips of his fin-gers. The question about what had happened to her was in his eyes; yet like Round Nose, he did not ask. Instead he moved behind her, put his hands under her arms, and lifted her onto the pinto.

"I too have something to say." Little Hawk positioned the reins on each side of the horse's neck and put the ends in her hands. "This horse is mine. I give him to you."

Walks Alone tried to hand the reins back, but Little Hawk stepped away. He raised a hand. "I have been on many raids with Victorio against the White Eyes and the Mexicans. I have taken other horses. This one"—he pointed at the pinto—"is best. Go and ride him to your grandmother."

Walks Alone watched her grandmother's face in the flickering light of their small campfire. The woman's face was grave, unreadable, and Walks Alone wondered what she was thinking.

Earlier, after the women had butchered a mule and readied camp for the night, the people had gathered around Walks Alone to hear her story. She'd been careful not to leave anything out— including the blame she put on herself for her brother's death. When she'd finished, everyone had dispersed. Her grandmother, who had seemed so happy upon first seeing her, hadn't spoken a word since.

A man coughed loudly, the customary signal when approaching another's campsite. Walks Alone turned to see Round Nose step through the fringe of firelight. He paid her no mind, focusing his attention on her grandmother.

The warrior stopped and folded his arms. "I have come from Little Hawk. He wishes to marry your granddaughter, Walks Alone. He is offering you much valuable property: four strong, fat ponies; four blankets; two knives; two buckskins; two Mexican saddles; and one long rope."

Walks Alone's eyes were wide in astonishment. A lump rose in her throat and she had to hold her hands together to keep them from trembling. A typical present to the relatives of a prospective bride was a blanket or two, a buckskin, and maybe a horse or a gun. *But four horses—saddles—knives.* Only a chief or extremely wealthy warrior could afford so much. Little Hawk had to be offering almost everything he owned.

Round Nose continued, his voice so serious that it almost sounded stern. "You know me, woman. You know that I do not lie. I have ridden many miles with Little Hawk. I have fought beside him. His wisdom is beyond his years. His words are true and his arrows fly straight. He will make a good husband for your granddaughter. He will provide well for you."

The elderly woman raised her head and looked at Round Nose for the first time. After a long moment the lines in her face relaxed and she spoke.

"Tell him his presents are generous. Tell him it is done. The marriage will take place three days after we are at Tres Castillos."

Round Nose turned sharply on his heel and left. Walks Alone rose and hurried to her grandmother, embracing her tightly.

The woman spoke. "My granddaughter, when you were away, you did nothing wrong. Your heart is good. Your deeds are honorable. I am proud of you. And now I am also happy. Soon I will have another grandchild to replace that which was lost."

CHAPTER FOURTEEN

———— ✦✦✦ ————

THE CARAVAN of Warm Springs Apaches was moving rapidly. Everyone was anxious to reach the lake of glistening water in the distance. Just beyond the lake were the three mountain peaks of Tres Castillos.

Walks Alone shifted her weight on the pinto. Little Hawk had been right about the horse. He was large boned and muscular, yet agile and quick, and he responded to the slightest pressure on the reins. She missed the colt she'd lost in the river, mostly because of the time she had spent with him. But he might never have become as good a horse as this one.

She glanced to the side at her grandmother, who was riding a small black horse. This made Walks Alone happy. No more would the woman walk wherever she went. The morning after Little Hawk's marriage proposal had been accepted, he had sent Round Nose with the promised presents. Walks Alone's grandmother was wealthy now. She had property to keep or to trade for whatever she needed.

Walks Alone gazed through the dust at the line of people in front of her. A few were mounted on horses, mules, or burros, but most were not so fortunate. They were all weary, and she was glad that soon they would have the opportunity to drink, bathe, and rest.

Her thoughts turned to Little Hawk. Because Victorio and the warriors were nearly out of ammunition, Little Hawk and a few other braves had left on a foray to try to find some. She wished he had not gone. He had told her he would be back by tomorrow night, but raids were always dangerous and often one or more warriors did not return.

She shook her head as if the action would clear away the troublesome notion. To think too much about something bad happening could cause it to happen. She must think only about Little Hawk's safe return and how happy they were going to be together.

Three more days. Walks Alone wished the marriage date had been set for sooner. Unless her grandmother decided to have a celebration feast, which was doubtful due to the scarcity of food, the only preparation needed was the building of a wickiup for the newly joined couple. And that, Walks Alone reasoned, shouldn't take them long.

Never again would Little Hawk and Walks Alone's grandmother purposely look upon one another. The Apache avoidance custom between a wife's relatives and her husband had to be strictly adhered to, even though their camps would henceforth be near each other. If either Little Hawk or her grandmother wanted to say something to the other, it would have to be done through Walks Alone or another messenger.

The wedding wouldn't take long. She and Little Hawk would simply enter their wickiup and begin their lives together.

Walks Alone watched as those in the front of the snakelike caravan reached the lake and began to spread out along its shore. She was happy, happier than she could ever remember. Here at Tres

Castillos, her life would soon be changed forever. She would be able to start a family.

A breeze blew in and Walks Alone saw a small, dusty whirlwind to her right. She remembered the last time she had seen one. It was after she had killed the rat, and before the band had been attacked in the canyon by Apache scouts. Again she wondered if the turbulent spiral might hold some kind of meaning.

Then something else caught her attention. Clouds of dust had covered a wide area against the horizon. She looked behind, then to her left. Everywhere was thick, dusty haze, except toward the lake. A storm was coming, she surmised. A windy, violent storm.

"Look!" she said to her grandmother, sweeping a hand around. Then specks became visible moving on the ground in front of the dust.

They were men. Mounted men. A whole army of them.

Others in the band saw the soldiers too. Soon everyone was rushing about in confusion, unsure of which way to go to escape.

Victorio and a group of warriors raced past. The chief shouted, his voice commandingly loud and clear, "Tres Castillos. The mountain peaks. Run to them."

Walks Alone stopped her horse and hastily helped a woman and her child mount behind her, then she followed her grandmother's horse at a hard gallop.

They skirted the lakeshore. The distance to the mountain peaks was fast closing.

All at once, seeming to come from nowhere, a line of Mexican soldiers appeared across their path. The soldiers' guns boomed in front of her. Walks Alone saw her grandmother tumble from her horse, saw the woman roll on the ground as her horse ran on.

Walks Alone slid the pinto to a halt and leaped off, handing the reins to the woman who remained on the horse.

"Take the horse. Go!"

Walks Alone hurried to her grandmother, who lay still. Blood from a bullet wound soaked the woman's neck. She was dead.

Bullets pitted the sand around Walks Alone. She dropped to the ground and leaned over her grandmother's body, wailing and rocking on her knees.

CHAPTER FIFTEEN

——◆✄◆——

WALKS ALONE'S HANDS were tied behind her back, the leather thong cutting deep into her wrists. A rope around her neck secured her to the captives in front of her and behind her. She stared at the ground as she plodded on, silently thanking Life Giver for keeping Little Hawk away and causing him to miss the battle.

The fighting had lasted all night, not stopping until early in the morning. But the Mexican soldiers had been too many. She knew that most of her people had been killed.

Walks Alone turned her head and looked back at the mountain peaks of Tres Castillos. Her family was gone, and so was her dream of a life with

Little Hawk. A single tear found its way down her face. She swallowed in an effort to choke back the flood that threatened to follow.

She lifted her chin. She was an Apache. Her captors would not see her cry.

EPILOGUE

———— ❈ ————

ON OCTOBER 15, 1880, Victorio and an estimated eighty-six of his warriors died at the Battle of Tres Castillos. The Mexican army took eighty-nine women and children captive. Many of these prisoners were taken to Mexico City and sold to large haciendas as house slaves and field hands. A few were eventually able to escape, make the long trek north on foot, and rejoin other Apache bands.

Although the outcome of the battle was a severe blow to the Apache nation, their fierce struggle for the freedom to live as their ancestors had was not over. There would be six more years of fighting before the last free band of Apaches, under the leadership of Geronimo and Chief Naiche, surrendered to the U.S. Army.

BIBLIOGRAPHY

Ball, Eve. *In the Days of Victorio*. James Kaywaykla, narrator. Tucson, Ariz.: University of Arizona Press, 1970.

———. *Indeh: An Apache Odyssey*. Provo, Utah: Brigham Young University Press, 1980.

Boyer, Ruth McDonald, and Narcissus Duffy Gayton. *Apache Mothers and Daughters*. Norman, Okla.: University of Oklahoma Press, 1992.

Goodwin, Grenville. *Western Apache Raiding and Warfare*. Tucson, Ariz.: University of Arizona Press, 1971.

Lockwood, Frank C. *The Apache Indians*. Lincoln, Nebr.: University of Nebraska Press, 1987 (first published 1938).

Opler, Morris E. *An Apache Life-Way*. Chicago: University of Chicago Press, 1941.

Reedstrom, Ernest Lisle. *Apache Wars: An Illustrated Battle History*. New York: Sterling Publishing, 1990.

Roberts, David. *Once They Moved Like the Wind*. New York: Simon & Schuster, 1993.

Sonnichsen, C. L. *The Mescalero Apaches*. Norman, Okla.: University of Oklahoma Press, 1958.

Stockel, H. Henrietta. *Women of the Apache Nation*. Reno, Nev.: University of Nevada Press, 1991.

Thrapp, Dan L. *Victorio and the Mimbres Apaches*. Norman and London, Okla.: University of Oklahoma Press, 1974.

Worcester, Donald E. *The Apaches: Eagles of the Southwest*. Norman, Okla.: University of Oklahoma Press, 1979.

ABOUT THE AUTHOR

Brian Burks is the author of several young adult novels, including *Runs With Horses, Soldier Boy,* and *Wrango,* all published by Harcourt. He has also written a series of classic westerns for adults. A man of many talents, Mr. Burks has worked as a range rider, cowboy, blacksmith, and ambulance driver. When he's not writing or riding his horse Banjo in the foothills of the Sacramento Mountains, he's probably tending the ranch or training horses. Mr. Burks lives with his wife and three youngest children in Tularosa, New Mexico.

More great books by Brian Burks

Runs With Horses

ALA Quick Pick
for Reluctant Young Adult Readers

New York Public Library Book
for the Teen Age

Soldier Boy

IRA Young Adults' Choice

Wrango